The True Stories of Ol' Melvin, Obadiah, Perkins MacGhee

and other Characters

by
Kenneth Lee McGee

For Everyone

Who Appreciates

A Good Yarn

These stories have been written over the course of several years though often quickly.
Some were written for my own amusement.
Others were written for family and friends.

Some of the stories are told by Grandpa Joseph Colasanti to his granddaughter Emmy. Some of them are from the point of view of the protagonist.
One begins with me sitting in a recliner.

Many of these adventures are adapted from the blogs on my website.

All are meant to be lighthearted entertainment.

Table of Contents

The Adventures Of Perkins MacGhee

The Ol' Melvin and Obadiah Stories

Tex Miller, the Last of the Singing Cowboys

Bonus

More Adventures of Rex Ford & Clay Horn

The Adventures of Perkins MacGhee

The Legend of Perkins MacGhee

—◆—

"Grandpa, can we walk over to the river?" Emmy asked. "It's not too hot and it's not super far to go since we're at Darby's."

"I suppose we can. Why do you want to see the river?" Grandpa asked as he finished his frosted mug of root beer.

"I just like to see it and watch the boats go by," eight-year-old Emmy answered. "Thanks for the root beer. It was yummy."

They returned their mugs to the counter and set out on their walk.

"I've been in there before," Emmy said pointing to a storefront.

"You have? When?" Grandpa asked noticing the iron bars over the windows of the pawnshop.

"Daddy brought me one time. He needed some money."

Grandpa shook his head. "That's no place for a child."

"I saw an electric piano and asked how much it cost. Daddy said it was too expensive."

They continued along the commercial street for several minutes. Emmy would run ahead of Grandpa Colasanti and peer inside the shops.

"Who were you waving at?" Grandpa asked.

"That's the lady who does Mom's hair."

"Has she ever cut yours?" Grandpa asked.

"Mom let her trim it last year," Emmy answered as she ran her fingers through her long ponytail. "Just a little. She

10

said I had split ends."

They crossed Broadmoor Avenue and turned to walk south.

"I know where we're going," Emmy said skipping ahead of Grandpa again. "There's a park over here where you can see the river."

A few minutes later they reached Pilchner Park.

"Can we go to the lookout and watch the boats?" Emmy asked.

Grandpa paused to catch his breath and waved for Emmy to go ahead. She dashed along the uphill gravel path that wound through the trees. She stopped when she heard the loud horn of one of the tugboats that pushed the barges up and down the river. When Grandpa arrived at the top of the bluff, Emmy was standing on the bottom rail of the wooden fence to get a better view.

"There are three boats going downriver, and I can see one over there waiting for them to pass," she said while pointing.

Grandpa gazed across the river, past the buildings of downtown South Hampshire to a bluff nearly a mile away.

"Do you know how the river got its name?" Emmy asked. "I've never heard of anything called Kinmundy before. It's a weird name."

Grandpa sat on the bench facing the river, removed his sweaty, baseball cap and ran a hand through his wiry gray hair. "According to the stories I've heard, it got its name from one of the early explorers who traveled up and down the river."

Emmy's eyes sparkled as she jumped jumped down from the railing and sat next to her grandfather. "Tell me more."

He squinted while following a plane heading toward the airport on the other side of the city, rubbed his jaw for a

11

moment and began, "Back in the late 1600s or so, this part of the country was pretty wild and unknown."

"Didn't they have maps?" Emmy interrupted.

Grandpa chuckled and said, "Not like we do today. Anyway, the only way people could get around was by canoe on the rivers, streams and lakes."

"Were there Indians?" she asked.

"I suppose so, because people have lived on the bluffs along the river for a long, long time. Sometimes they would exchange goods with the traders who were brave enough to get to know the natives. According to local legend, one of the traders was named Perkins MacGhee."

Emmy turned on the bench to face her grandfather. She put her hands under her knees and gazed into his eyes. "What was he like?"

"He was a giant of a man. Several inches over six feet tall with long flowing hair under a hat made from beaver hides and he had a full, bushy beard. He dressed in animal skins and spoke in a strange language."

Emmy inched closer.

"MacGhee came from Scotland to seek his fortune. No one knows just why or how he got to this area, but he traded with the Indians for several years. He would come and go up and down the river. He would camp along the far side." Grandpa stood up and pointed to the east. "Can you see where the land rises?"

Emmy stood up and peered across the valley. "I think I can."

"Thousands, or maybe millions of years ago, all that land was under a large lake. The river might have been a lot wider, too." He sat down and continued, "So this MacGhee decided to name the river after the place where he grew up. Loch Kinmundy. Loch means lake in Scottish, and this is the only place with that name as far as I know."

Emmy stood up for a moment longer as two of the boats were passing each other. "I thought they were going to crash into each other. They get so close."

"Once in a great while, they do collide. I remember one time when some barges collided and they sank to the bottom of the river. The river was closed until they could be salvaged."

"What does that mean?" Emmy asked.

"They had to repair the barges so they would float again," he explained. "Anyway, MacGhee named this the Kinmundy River to remind him of his home in Scotland, and the name has stuck for all these years."

"Whatever happened to him?" she asked after sitting down.

Grandpa smiled and said, "That's where the story gets interesting."

Emmy's eyes sparkled again.

"According to the legend handed down over the generations, one spring day MacGhee was heading down the river with a load of goods, and he kinda disappeared into the mist. Poof! He vanished into the fog. None of the locals ever saw him again, but they did find an empty canoe several weeks later. It had washed up on the island that's just before the big highway bridge."

"Did he drown? Did some mean people get him? Didn't he know how to swim? I know how."

Grandpa shrugged. "No one knows for sure, but they never found a body, or any of the goods he was carrying." Grandpa paused, and when he started again, his voice was just above a whisper, "This is where it gets spooky. Over the years, whenever there's a lot of fog and mist on the river, some of the boat captains swear they've seen a giant, bearded man in old-fashioned animal skins paddling a loaded canoe in and out of the mist."

"Are you making that up, Grandpa?" she asked sitting up and crossing her arms over her chest.

He waved a finger, shook his head and said, "I'm not making it up, sweetheart. That's the true story of how the river got its name and the origin of the legend of Perkins MacGhee."

The Capture of Perkins MacGhee

—◆—

"Emmy, I remembered another story about Perkins MacGhee. Would you like to hear it?" Grandpa Colasanti asked while they were weeding Grandma's flower bed.

Emmy wiped some dirt from her hands onto her shorts and nodded. "Can we take a break and drink some lemonade? I'm really thirsty."

"I think Grandma made some earlier," he answered.

A few minutes later they sat on the porch swing and drank their iced lemonade.

"What else happened to Perkins MacGhee?" Emmy asked as her eyes sparkled.

"This occurred many years before MacGhee paddled down the Kinmundy River right past where SoHam is today." Grandpa took a long drink of lemonade, then continued, "MacGhee was trapping beavers and kept finding rivers that took him farther and farther north and west."

"In Canada?" Emmy asked.

"Yes! He was exploring parts of Canada where no European had ever been. Only the natives called The First People lived in this area. It was mostly flat with many rivers and lakes. There were times when MacGhee had to carry his canoe around rapids and steep waterfalls." Grandpa paused.

"The Kinmundy River has a waterfall right here in SoHam. I like to go there and feel the spray on my face."

"MacGhee spent three years exploring this new land. He collected many pelts and saw new creatures. He saw a moose for the first time. The moose was taller than MacGhee with antlers as wide as MacGhee could stretch his arms. At first he was afraid and was about to shoot it, but he realized the moose wouldn't harm him."

"That's good."

"So, MacGhee left the moose alone. He came across black bears and elk and sheep with huge horns. He forged his way west until he came to the highest mountains he had ever seen. They were covered in snow as far as the eye could see. He had to leave his canoe behind and walk. Often the snow would be falling and the wind blowing so hard he couldn't see five feet in front of him. One time he was struggling through a blizzard and heard the loud call of a moose. He stood absolutely still for a moment and then suddenly the wind stopped and the snow quit falling. He could see where he was."

"Where was he, Grandpa?" Emmy asked.

"He was at the edge of a thousand foot cliff. If he had taken another step, he would have fallen to his death."

"Oh, my!" Emmy put a hand to her mouth. "Was it the same moose he had seen before?"

"I'm pretty sure it was, sweetie. Anyway, he climbed up and down for many weeks until he came to the edge of a large body of water."

"Was it the ocean?" she asked. "He must have discovered the Pacific Ocean. He was probably in British Columbia. I've seen pictures of it in a library book and it is beautiful."

"That's exactly where he was," Grandpa said.

Grandma came out and refilled their lemonade.

"Grandpa is telling me another story," Emmy said.

"He is, huh?" Grandma rolled her eyes. "My flower beds won't weed themselves."

"Okay, so while MacGhee was looking at the ocean, some natives surrounded him. They had never seen a person like MacGhee before. He was much taller..."

"And his skin was white. Theirs was probably a lot darker, huh?"

"It was. They bound MacGhee using ropes made from buffalo hide and carried him to their camp. The chiefs held a pow wow to determine what to do with him. One of the chiefs suggested they feed him to the wolves. Another thought he was sent from their ancestors and they should worship him. The bravest of the native people offered to fight a battle and let him win his freedom."

"I bet I know what happened," Emmy said with a grin.

"Obviously, the native people didn't murder him, but this is what really happened."

Emmy took another drink of lemonade and gave her full attention to Grandpa.

"They decided to set MacGhee free and let the bravest of all the warriors search for him. If he escaped, he would go free. If he was caught, he would have to work for the natives the rest of his life." Grandpa paused, took a drink and collected his thoughts. "The day came and by using sign language the natives made MacGhee understand what was going to happen. They set him free and MacGhee shook hands with all the warriors and then walked into the deep forest. He was allowed a thirty minute head start before the bravest warrior would pursue him. MacGhee disappeared into the woods, but he didn't go very far."

"Why not? Didn't he know the warrior was after him?"

"He knew, but he had a plan."

Emmy's eyes opened wider.

"He planned to hide until dark and return to camp and steal..."

"It's not right to steal, Grandpa."

"He borrowed the biggest canoe he could find and escaped. He paddled along the coastline by night and hid during the day for over a week until he knew he was safe. He kept going south and discovered trees that were five hundred feet tall. He came upon strange rock formations at the edge of the great ocean. Later, he came upon a bay with a golden bridge. He kept going south and found some wild horses. He had never seen a horse before before. He talked to it, gained its trust and jumped on its back. He left the canoe behind and rode the horse straight toward the rising sun. For weeks he traveled across deserts and mountains and then prairies. Finally, he arrived at the bank of a mighty river. He set the horse free and made a canoe. He sailed, I mean, he paddled up the river until he came to another river that headed into the rising sun again."

"He was going east, huh?" Emmy pointed in that direction.

"Yes, and after three more months, and several close calls with more native people, MacGhee made it back to where he had started."

"What did he do with all the beaver pelts, Grandpa?"

Grandpa tilted his head then rubbed his jaw. "Oh, he traded those for food back in Canada. That way he was able to explore easier."

"Did he ever get captured again?"

Grandpa grinned and raised a hand. "That's the interesting part of the story. Remember the warrior that was chasing MacGhee earlier?"

"I remember."

"Well, he didn't give up. He kept finding clues about where Perkins MacGhee had been."

"Did he find him and capture him?"

"The warrior and MacGhee did meet again. They recognized each other immediately, but instead of fighting, they became best friends."

"That's good. Did the warrior have a name?"

"He did!" Grandpa exclaimed. "I can't pronounce his native people name, but it meant One-Who-Rides-The-Sun." He looked around the yard, spotted a rose plant and then leaned closer to Emmy. He whispered in her ear, "MacGhee gave the warrior a new name. It was Thornbush and for many years MacGhee and Thornbush explored the land from the Gulf of Mexico all the way to the frozen land north of Canada."

"Ahem," Grandma said with hands on hips, "I appreciate a good story as much as the next person, but I still want my flowers beds weeded."

"I suppose we better get back to work, Grandpa. Maybe you can tell me more about Perkins MacGhee and Thornbush after supper."

The Spirit of Perkins MacGhee

—◆—

"Can you tell me more about Perkins MacGhee and Thornbush now, Grandpa?"

"Yes, I have the time if you give me a minute to collect my thoughts."

"You can take your time, Grandpa."

"Let's sit on the swing, and I'll tell you how Perkins MacGhee and Thornbush traveled all the way to the North Pole."

"The North Pole! Did they really go that far?" she asked.

"Well, maybe they didn't make it exactly to the pole, but they went farther north than any other men in history. They started out by trapping beavers and trading the pelts for food and things they needed. They kept heading north through wild country where not even the native people lived because there was no food or any trees to build a shelter. At first they rode horses, but the weather was so cold the horses froze to death."

"Oh, poor horseys."

"They kept going until they came to what looked like another ocean except this one was filled with icebergs larger than the tallest building in SoHam. They fashioned canoes out of animal hide and what little wood they could find. They made their way in and around the icebergs. Every once in a while they would hear a loud crack and large parts of the icebergs would break off and crash into the water. A few times they were almost tipped over by the waves, but they stayed upright. For more months than they could remember, the kept going. Every so often they would spot land. They would paddle hard and make it to shore. They would search for food and sometimes they would have to dig for roots under the snow and ice. Thornbush taught MacGhee how to fish through the ice, so they could always catch fish to eat. They would use the fish bones as needles to repair the hides they wore as clothes. They saw strange animals swimming in the ocean that looked like fat sausages with stumpy legs that would waddle onto the land at times."

"Were they seals and walruses?" Emmy asked.

"They probably were. They would catch some of these animals if they needed their skin to make new shoes and the fat they used to make enough oil to light their lanterns."

Emmy tilted her head.

"They made primitive forms of what we call lanterns. One day they were on a different island when they saw thousands of birds come out of the ocean and waddle onto the snow. They looked different than any other birds they had ever seen. They were black and white and looked like they were dressed up to go to a fancy party."

"They were penguins, Grandpa."

"Yes, but they didn't know that back then. They caught one of the birds and tried to eat it, but it tasted terrible, so they left them alone." Grandpa laughed for a moment. "That's why people don't eat penguins like they do chicken or ducks or geese. They taste terrible. Only whales and maybe sharks eat them now."

"I wouldn't want to even try one."

"Finally, they got to a point where all they could see was ice mountains. They decided to turn around before they starved to death. They were getting ready to leave when they saw three huge white bears. Since they had never seen a white bear before, they thought they were seeing the spirits of dead bears. This frightened them so much, they took off right away. They left behind the last of their food."

"Why? Didn't they know they would get hungry?"

"They were so afraid of the spirit bears they had to get away. They figured they could survive on fish and whatever small game they could trap. They kept going for months and months. Eventually they came upon a house made of ice and found some friendly natives."

"Grandpa! How can anyone live in a house made of ice? Wouldn't it melt if you made a fire in the fireplace?"

"I don't think they had fireplaces or anyway to heat the ice house. They lived with these people for over a year. They learned how to speak their language and taught the native people a few words of their own."

"What language did MacGhee and Thornbush speak, Grandpa?"

"MacGhee came from the far north of what is called Scotland. He spoke the ancient language he learned as a child. Thornbush spoke several different Indian dialects and had taught MacGhee how to speak them, too."

"They must have been really smart. I only know a few words in Italian because sometimes Mom and Daddy yell at each other that way so we can't understand them."

"One night they were all sitting outside when MacGhee spoke about the white spirit bears. He had been too afraid to mention them before because he thought the natives would think he was crazy and send him away to be lost in the snow and ice. He was surprised when the natives told stories about seeing the spirit bears many years ago."

"Did the white bears ever travel south to where these people lived?"

"Only if they were desperate for food. The oldest native told a story his ancestors had told to their children down through the ages. He spoke of a time when there were giant animals that swam in the oceans and only came to the surface when they needed to spout water high into the air."

"Those are whales," Emmy said. "I've seen them at the big aquarium in the city."

"The old man talked about a time when the white bears traveled south and caught seals to eat. He said the men would hunt for the bears in large groups and use their fur to make clothes. Then the men would be like spirits when they hunted other animals because they would wear white hides that camouflaged them. Eventually, the bears learned to stay far to the north and avoid the native people."

Grandpa stopped and took a deep breath.

"Are you okay?" Emmy asked.

"Yes, I just needed to pause a minute. I'm okay. Where was I?"

"MacGhee and Thornbush were living with the natives in the ice house."

"Right, the oldest native decided to show MacGhee one of the old hides the hunters used to wear. Since MacGhee and Thornbush had been such good friends to the natives, they gave each of them a white, spirit bear hide to wear to stay warm. MacGhee and Thornbush thanked the natives and decided to move south where the weather was warmer and there was more game to catch and more natives to trade pelts with. They eventually reached what they thought was another ocean, but it's what we call Lake Superior. They built canoes because there were now lots of trees. They paddled across the lake, found land, crossed it and then found a longer lake. That's Lake Michigan now. They paddled south stopping at different Indian settlements. One time they stopped at the site of unfriendly Indians."

"Did those Indians try to shoot them with arrows?" she asked while pretending to shoot an arrow.

23

"They did, but MacGhee and Thornbush managed to get away even though there were six or seven canoes filled with hostile Indians after them. They escaped when a storm caused the lake to get mad and send waves over twenty feet high at them. The Indians headed back, but MacGhee and Thornbush had to keep going. They survived the storm, but lost all their gear except for the bear hides. They kept going and put ashore at a swamp they thought smelled like wild onions." He paused to see if Emmy knew where they were. But she didn't say anything. "There they found friendly Indians and were able to gather some corn and squash the Indians grew. The Indians shared their food with MacGhee and Thornbush who thanked them by showing the Indians how to capture the wild turkeys."

"Is that how Thanksgiving started?"

"Not really, but it was kind of like that. MacGhee and Thornbush found the mouth of a new river and paddled south. That river led to another and then another. Soon they were here in SoHam, but of course it wasn't called that then. They came ashore just where the Kinmundy River makes that bend to the west and they climbed the high bluffs. All they could see for miles was tall prairie grass and trees. They saw the waterfall and figured they would have to carry their canoes around it. When they got back to the river, they heard some unfriendly Indians coming and shooting arrows at them. They had to jump in their canoes and head down the river to escape. Since the water was cold, they put on the white bear hides. The unfriendly natives saw this and slowed down. MacGhee and Thornbush saw the unfriendly natives pointing at them and figured the spirit bear hides scared them. They were going to stop, but the current was too strong. No matter how hard they paddled, the river kept pushing them toward the falls. They tried and tried to make it to the shore, but the river wouldn't let them."

"Oh, no! Those falls are huge! I've stood right by them."

"They could hear the falls ahead, so they paddled as hard as they could. They got to the edge and sailed into the air while the friendly natives watched from on top of the bluff. MacGhee and Thornbush landed at the bottom of the falls without hitting any of the rocks. The natives watched them paddle away and told everyone they met the story of the two spirits who could fly through the air in canoes and survive the river waterfalls. After that the legend of Perkins MacGhee and Thornbush was told down the years."

The Lost Treasure of Perkins MacGhee

—◆—

Emmy held Grandpa's hand as they walked up the hill to Pilchner Park. When they arrived at the top of the bluff, Emmy stood on the bottom wooden rail of the fence to get a better view.

"Did I thank you for the ice cream, Grandpa?" Eight-year-old Emmy asked while staring down at the Kinmundy River.

"Yes, you did and you are most welcome," Grandpa answered wiping the sweat from his forehead.

"Do you know anymore stories about Perkins MacGhee?" she asked waving at one of the tugboats.

Grandpa rubbed the wiry, gray stubble of his beard and tilted his head. "I might know another story."

"Tell me, Grandpa!" Emmy squealed jumping off the fence and facing him.

Grandpa sat on the bench facing the river and tried to remember the first story he told her about the legendary fur trapper and explorer who had given the river its name. He chuckled as he recalled the story about the ghost who would appear out of the mist. "I can remember a story my father told me a long time ago about a lost treasure."

Emmy sat on the bench facing her grandfather. She put her hands under her knees and gazed into his eyes. "You have to tell me."

"You remember MacGhee was a giant of a man. Several inches over six feet tall with long flowing hair under a hat made from beaver hides and had a full bushy beard. He dressed in animal skins and spoke in a strange language, right?"

Emmy nodded as her eyes sparkled.

"Well, the story is that MacGhee was exploring high in the mountains of... uh... Michigan in the middle of winter. The snow was coming down so fast he couldn't see his hands in front of his face."

"Did he have a sled? I like to slide down Windsor Hill if there's enough snow."

"I don't think he had a sled, but he managed to find a cave high up near the top of the mountain. He stepped inside to get out of the snow. There was a stone ledge so he set his backpack down and decided to make the cave his camp until the snow stopped."

"I like to go camping. It's fun to sleep in a tent and I don't get scared," she said proudly.

Grandpa smiled recalling the time Emmy camped in the backyard.

"When the snow stopped, MacGhee gathered some firewood, started a fire at the mouth of the cave and made his supper."

"What did he eat? Did he make soup or SpagettiOs?"

"I think he made a rabbit stew with potatoes and carrots and a wild onion," Grandpa answered. He stared at a hawk flying overhead for a moment. "He ended up staying in the cave the whole winter because there was so much snow. He would trap rabbits and once even shot a..."

"Don't tell me he shot a baby deer, Grandpa!" Emmy interrupted waving her hands.

"It wasn't a deer. It was a vicious wolverine."

"What's that?"

"It's sorta like a small bear that is mean to other animals. Anyway, MacGhee survived on the animals and berries he found just outside the cave." Grandpa nodded several times. "He ate lots of blueberries and found an apple tree with yellow apples."

"I would rather eat spaghetti with meatballs unless they're made with those bear things."

"He probably ran out of pasta," Grandpa said with a laugh. "Finally, it stopped snowing enough for the sun to come out. MacGhee decided to explore deeper into the cave and guess what he found."

"What?"

"He found more gold and silver than he could dream of. Right there in plain sight."

"What did he do with it?"

"He used his hammer to get all of the gold and silver and put it into his backpack. Then he waited until it was spring and was going to go down the mountain back to his house in town."

"Grandpa! I thought he didn't have a house because he lived in a canoe."

"Right you are!" Grandpa pointed at her while nodding. "I meant the shelter made of trees where he stored his canoe when he wasn't using it. So, he was getting ready to break camp. He stuffed everything into his backpack and took one last look around the cave. Just as he was ready to walk out he heard something rustling near the back of the cave."

"What was it?"

Grandpa stood up, spread his arms wide and made a growling noise. "It was a huge black bear just waking up."

Emmy giggled, rolled her eyes and then asked, "Didn't he know about the bear?"

Grandpa rubbed his jaw. "No, he couldn't see it because it was in a corner where the light didn't reach. He stood still for a moment. The huge bear stood up and filled the entire cave it was so big. MacGhee knew the bear would be hungry after sleeping all winter but he wasn't afraid. The bear yawned and stretched his arms for a moment. Then it spotted MacGhee."

Emmy leaned back against the bench and wrapped her arms around her chest.

"MacGhee and the bear were only a few feet apart but neither one moved for a long time. MacGhee stared into the bear's eyes and slowly... as slow as really cold pancake syrup... began to turn away. The bear sniffed the backpack and detected the smell of the food MacGhee had packed."

"I thought it was full of gold and silver?"

"Yes, but there was room for just enough food to get back down to... his canoe."

"Okay, go on."

"Once the bear realized there was food in the backpack, he raised a paw that was bigger than that rock over there." Grandpa pointed to a decorative stone about the size of a basketball.

"What did MacGhee do?"

"Well, the bear ripped the backpack away and tried to take a bite. MacGhee turned to face the bear and grabbed his trusty rifle."

"Did they really have guns back then? You told me this was like four hundred years ago in the first story."

"He had a homemade gun."

Emmy tilted her head back and forth as she ran a finger through her ponytail. "Okay, I suppose he could have made a gun."

"MacGhee only had a second to save his life, so he pulled the trigger and shot the bear in the stomach. The bear roared and MacGhee fired again. The cave started shaking because the gun and the bear made so much noise it caused an earthquake. The cave began to collapse." Grandpa waved his arms and stomped his feet. "Parts of the ceiling came down in huge chunks. MacGhee turned and ran for the opening just as the entire cave collapsed."

"Did he get the backpack?"

Grandpa stood still. Then he shook his head. "All the snow on the mountain began to come down."

"There was an avalanche, huh?"

"Yes. MacGhee curled up into a ball and rolled all the way down the mountain along with all the snow and trees and rocks. When he hit the bottom he had to dig his way out of six, no, twenty feet of snow. He popped his head through the snow, took a deep breath and looked up." Grandpa stared into the sky.

"What did he see?" Emmy asked standing up next to Grandpa.

"All he could see was an ocean of white. The snow and avalanche had obliterated... uh... changed the entire mountain. There weren't any trees or rocks or anything left. All he could see was a sheet of white without any trace of a cave."

"So, the avalanche completely covered the cave with the dead bear inside, huh?"

"Yep! There was no trace of the cave or the bear."

"Or the gold and silver."

Grandpa nodded. "The snow didn't melt that summer, and more snow fell in the winter. In fact, there has been snow on that mountain ever since. It just keeps getting deeper and deeper. No matter how hard MacGhee, or anyone tried, they could never find the cave again."

"So, that's why it's a lost treasure, huh, Grandpa?" She took his hand and they started walking down the hill.

"Until this very day there is a cave filled with gold and silver..."

"And a humongous dead bear," she added. "That's a pretty good story, Grandpa, but..."

Grandpa stopped suddenly, let go of Emmy's hand, put his hands on his knees and faced her. His eyes were wide open. "There's more. You see that mountain is where people go skiing now and sometimes when there are too many people trying to ski, the people stop and swear they can hear something roaring from deep under the snow near the top of the mountain. They claim they can hear scraping noises like something trying to escape. They say it sounds like a bear is getting closer and closer to the top of the snow."

Emmy stared up at Grandpa. "Are you making that up?"

"You have to decide for yourself." Grandpa put an arm around her shoulders and squeezed as they began walking again. "It's just another of the legends of Perkins MacGhee."

The Legacy of Perkins MacGhee

—◆—

"Grandpa, will you help me write a story about Perkins MacGhee and Thornbush? I want to show my teacher and get extra credit."

Grandpa turned off the hose he was using to water Grandma's flowers. "You want to write a story, huh?"

"Yes! And I want you to read it when I finish. Will you?"

"Of course, Emmy."

She dashed around the house and sat at the picnic table in the sun. She tapped her pencil against her chin, grinned and started to write.

Perkins MacGhee was born in Loch Kinmundy, Scotland back in the early 1600s. He left his home because he wanted to explore the new world. He became a trapper and traveled up and down all the rivers of this country in a canoe. Along the way he had many adventures. He met an Indian that he called Thornbush, who shared his adventures for many years. He and Thornbush paddled their canoes down the Kinmundy River and other rivers in the area.

Emmy checked her story and tried to think of more to write. She kicked her feet back and forth under the table and listened to some birds squawking. She tapped her pencil on the table, but couldn't think of anything else to write about.

"I'll show this to Grandpa, and maybe he can help me think of more to write."

She raced around the house, waving her paper. "Grandpa, I need help. I don't know what else to write."

He read her little story, tapped his chin and said, "I know something else he did I haven't told you. You can use it for your story."

"Okay."

They sat on the front porch steps. Grandpa stretched out his legs and shrugged his shoulders until they popped.

"MacGhee and Thornbush escaped the unfriendly tribe that chased him down the river. Then he and Thornbush followed the river as it went west for a ways then south and then back west. Another river joined it and it became even wider than it is here in SoHam. That river is what we call the Illinois River today. They followed this river until they came to a place with high sandstone cliffs. The river became narrower and had to go around both sides of a mysterious island. On one side of the island were rapids that looked too dangerous to go through. But the other side was a little wider and the water was calmer. There was only one problem."

"What was that?"

"There was a waterfall at the end of the calm water. One even bigger than the falls in SoHam."

"What dd they do?"

"They couldn't get out of the river because of the cliffs, so they had to shoot through the rapids. They took off and zoom! They were going faster than ever before. They had to push against some boulders and a minute later, they were in calm water again. They paddled to the shore in an opening of the cliff and made camp. They found a way to climb to the top of the bluff and looked out at the river. They hiked down a ways and could then see the falls much easier. MacGhee told Thornbush they never would have survived going over that waterfall."

"Didn't they still have their white, spirit bear coats?"

"Yes, but it was too hot to wear them."

"It must have been in the summer, huh?"

"I think so. They stayed in the area long enough to hunt for some... wild turkeys and..."

"It's okay if you tell me they killed deer to eat. I know people have to eat to survive."

"They only killed what they needed and left the rest of the deer alone. For a few days they stayed in their camp along the river. At night they would hear coyotes and wolves and even an occasional mountain lion."

"There aren't any mountains here."

"No, but there used to be large wildcats that lived in the forests and only hunted at night. They're all gone now, but this was four hundred years ago. There weren't any roads or real towns or anything other than animal trails. They decided to keep following the river and after several days they came to the mighty Mississippi River. Of course it didn't have a name then. They followed that river..."

"South, right?" Emmy asked impatiently.

Grandpa shook his head. "You would think they would go that way, but they didn't. They paddled upstream against the current."

"Wasn't that hard to do?"

"Mighty hard, but they kept to the banks where it was easier, but also more dangerous because they were closer to any unfriendly natives that way. They traveled as far north as they could until the mighty river became just a little creek that you could step across. By now it was winter and they needed to make a shelter or else they would freeze to death. They remembered how the native people in Canada used snow to make houses, so that's what they did. They created the first igloo in this country. You could put that in your story, Emmy. It's like their legacy."

The Final Adventure of Perkins MacGhee

—◆—

"Do you know how Perkins MacGhee and Thornbush died, Grandpa?" Emmy asked. "I told my teacher I would write a report about it."

Grandpa put down his newspaper and turned down the TV volume. "No one knows exactly how it happened. Some legends say he drowned in the river. Others swear he lived for fifty more years up in Canada. I even heard another story about his last great adventure with Thornbush."

"Tell me, please."

He patted a spot next to him on the couch. Emmy sat close and snuggled against him. She loved the smell of his aftershave.

"This is what I believe happened to Perkins MacGhee and his Indian companion Thornbush. They had been exploring all over the country for over forty years. All the way from the end of the Mississippi River to close to the North Pole. They went from the Atlantic Ocean to the Pacific and almost every place in between where there was a waterway. The only place they had never been was to a big island far to the east. Some sailors from Denmark, I believe, had discovered it and named it Greenland."

"Was it covered in grass and trees?"

Grandpa grinned and shook his head. "Just the opposite. It was completely covered in ice several hundred feet thick. MacGhee and Thornbush made a bigger canoe and loaded it with enough food for over a year. Then they set off for this mysterious island."

35

"Did they get there?"

"No one knows for sure, but I believe they did. I think they made it to the island and landed on the only place they could find to climb onto the glaciers. They hauled their canoe up the side of the cliff for almost fifty feet. They got to the top and all they could see for miles was snow and ice. They didn't know how big this island was, but they figured they get walk across it because they were wearing snowshoes that allowed them to stay on top of the snow. The only landmark they could see was a thin smoke signal far away."

"You mean like an Indian smoke signal?"

"No, this was like the smoke from really hot water." Grandpa laughed and said, "It was a steam signal. They kept the signal in sight as they made their way across the snow and ice for days. They didn't know it but they were going higher and higher all the time."

"Like climbing a mountain, huh?"

"Kinda like that, but a mountain is steeper. This was like a prairie of snow and ice that gradually rose higher."

"I see."

"They traveled for over a week and didn't seem to be any closer. They were now at the point where they had to make a decision. They had reached the point of no return!"

"What does that mean?"

"It meant they had just enough provisions left to maybe make it back to their canoe, or if they kept going and didn't find food soon, they might stave to death."

"Which way did they go? I bet I know."

"What do you think?"

"They were brave explorers so I think they kept going. Am I right?"

"Yes, you are. They didn't even consider turning back. They were down to their last little bit of old bread when they finally reached the top of a ridge. They looked out and could see where the thin column of smoke came from over a thousand feet below."

"Where? Was it a volcano?"

"It was! Right in the middle of this oasis of green was a volcano that rose up and the smoke came from there. They could see trees and grass and water on all sides of the circular volcano. The volcano was covered in black rock. They tried to circle around the ridge to find a way into the land around the volcano, but they couldn't find one. They were almost back to where they started when MacGhee spotted a mountain goat walking along a ledge that wasn't any wider than the radiator behind us."

Emmy turned around and looked over the couch at the small radiator. "That's not very wide."

"No, but it was the only way into the oasis."

"What exactly does oasis mean?"

"In the desert there are places where there's water and trees grow around it. That's what it means."

"Okay."

"They had to leave everything behind except for the clothes on their backs."

"Were they wearing the white bear coats?"

"Yes! They were and they watched those goats make their way down into the oasis. They shook hands and took off. They followed the narrow path as it went deeper and deeper into the oasis. They knew that one false step would mean falling to their death, but they kept going."

"Because they would have starved to death otherwise, right?"

Grandpa nodded. "After three days on the treacherous path it finally widened enough so they could relax a little. By now they could see native people living in huts made of grass and mud. The people saw them and came to see who they were. You see no one had ever made it down the trail in over a thousand years. MacGhee and Thornbush were the first explorers any of these people had ever seen. When they saw their white coats, they thought they were the spirits of the bears who had once live on the island, and they were afraid. MacGhee was the first to approach them. He took off the coat and let them see he was a human just like them except he was two feet taller then the tallest one."

"Did they think he was a giant?"

"Actually, they thought he was a god. The god of their ancestors who worshiped the great white bears so long ago that only a faint memory remained. They took MacGhee to a cave on the side of the volcano, and inside was an ancient picture of a great white bear and another of the top of the mountain with fire coming out."

"That must have been when the volcano erupted and formed the big crater they were in."

"You are right, Emmy. Over the years the sides of the crater eroded into steep cliffs which trapped everyone. No one was able to climb the steep cliffs."

"But MacGhee and Thornbush made it down."

"Yes, because it was easier to go down than to try and climb up the trail. There were sections where the trail had gaps and these people weren't tall enough to cross those gaps. Since MacGhee and Thornbush had longer legs, they could leap across the gaps and go down the trail. But even they would have a difficult time getting out of the crater."

"Do you think they ever made it out, Grandpa?"

"No one can say for sure, but scientists today have learned that around 1675 or so, there was a huge eruption on Greenland. It was so big and there was so much lava and rocks and ash that it filled the entire crater that had been there before. Since that time the snow and ice have obliterated any sign of the volcano and it crater. That volcano now lies under several hundred feet of sow and ice. It's so big that the people who visit the shores of Greenland can see it. They even gave it a name."

"What did they name it?" she asked with eyes that sparkled.

"They call it by a native name that means 'land of the sleeping white bear."

"Does anyone live there today?"

"No one lives anywhere close to the top of the mountain. To the natives it is sacred ground, and to the other people it is haunted."

"So no one ever knew if MacGhee and Thornbush ever left the island, huh?"

"There was never any proof they made it off the island, but if you listen to the stories told by really old people who live on the eastern shore of Canada, they have a legend of two white bears who landed on the shore covered in dark ash."

Emmy grinned and dashed to the dining room table. "Thanks, Grandpa. I got to write about that. My teacher will love that story."

The
Ol' Melvin
and
Obadiah
Stories

Part 1

—◆—

"Sorry, Emmy, but I don't know any other stories about Perkins MacGhee," Grandpa said. He rubbed his jaw for a moment and then grinned. "I do know a story about a gold prospector and two cowboys."

"I don't care about cowboys," Emmy whined as she hopped over a crack in the sidewalk. "You don't have to go for a walk if you're too tired. It is rather hot."

"It's typical for August and I need the exercise. Your mother is gossiping with Grandma about her sister and everyone she knows in SoHam and I don't want to listen to it." Grandpa waved at one of his neighbors. "The cowboys were outlaws and tried to rob an old man. Does that make a difference?"

"Sure." Emmy looked up at Grandpa to see if his eyes gave away anything about this story, but his expression didn't change. "I like to hear your stories."

"Well, the story takes place in Wyoming around 1890. There were these two outlaws that had a hideout up in the mountains outside of this mining town named..." He paused for a moment while staring at one of the neighbor's houses. "The town was called Polanka Flats." He hoped Emmy didn't know the name of the people who lived in the house they were passing. "Polanka Flats was a boomtown because of the gold found by a prospector named Melvin Boyd." Grandpa waved to another neighbor. "Boyd traveled all over the western territories and was a typical prospector of the day except for one thing."

42

"What thing?" Emmy asked after Grandpa paused again.

"Boyd had a glass eye and a stubborn ol' donkey he called Obadiah. Boyd and Obadiah had been prospecting all over the West for close to fifty years."

"Grandpa, can donkeys live that long?"

He shook his head. "Not normally, but Obadiah was an exception to the rule. Anyway, Ol' Melvin and Obadiah made their way into the Wyoming mountains late in the fall of 1889. There wasn't a town there yet, but they made camp and started digging in the side of Doolen Mountain."

"How did he know where to dig? Was there a sign that said 'Dig here for gold'?" Emmy giggled after asking her question.

Grandpa shook his head. "No, he just had a feeling. Anyway, a couple of weeks later they struck it rich. Ol' Melvin started whoopin' and hollerin' for all he was worth. He fired his rusty old Robnett rifle at a big boulder but missed it. Even Obadiah knew somethin' was up and started hopping up and down and braying like donkeys do. Melvin dug out enough ore to fill up the saddlebags and he disguised the opening to the mine. Then he and Obadiah headed down Doolen Mountain to the nearest town which was called Soldnerville. They went to the place where they could get the ore tested and the ore turned out to be full of gold and even had some silver in it. Ol' Melvin tried to keep calm, but he kinda got a bit carried away. He took Obadiah to one one of the saloons and tied him to the hitchin' post. The saloon was run by a man with a handlebar mustache and slicked-back, oily black hair named Streak Garrett. Ol' Melvin bought a bottle of cheap whiskey and stood at the bar. After consuming a few glasses of the cheap rotgut liquor, he started tellin' Ivan Hanna, the bartender, about how he was gonna become the richest man in all of Wyoming."

43

"That wasn't very smart of him, huh?" Emmy asked while they waited at the corner.

Grandpa shook his head. "The bartender nodded to two men who worked in the saloon as cardsharps, but who in reality were outlaws. Their names were Lonesome Bill Broom and One-Eyed Jack Mahan and they were the most lowdown outlaws in the whole territory."

"Did he really only have one eye? You said that the old prospector only had one eye."

Grandpa rubbed his jaw. "Yeah, I did because back in the old west a lot of men lost their eyes because of the dust in the mines and the desert," Grandpa explained hoping it would pass Emmy's muster. "So these two outlaws plotted with Streak Garrett to follow Ol' Melvin and Obadiah when they left town. They followed them up the mountain and found out where the gold was. Then they headed back to Soldner to tell their boss.

Emmy stared up at Grandpa, but didn't interrupt his story.

"Now Ol' Melvin and Obadiah knew they better get all the gold they could out of their claim before someone tried to rob it from them. He kept diggin' out the ore where he could see there was gold. Then in the middle of the night, he loaded up Obadiah and they headed out of Polanka City. When they were a mile or so down the mountain, Lonesome Bill Broom and One-Eyed Jack Mahan ambushed them and stole all the gold. They conked Ol' Melvin over the head and left him for dead. Then they hightailed it back to town and put all the gold in the local bank and swore to Bert Geiler, who ran the bank and the general store, that they mined the gold themselves. Now Geiler was a smart man and had heard about Ol' Melvin's strike. He knew the outlaws were lyin' through their teeth, but he locked the gold in the vault and after they left he telegraphed Sheriff Glen Johnson and told him everything."

"Can we stop for ice cream, please?"

"We can stop."

Emmy grinned and let Grandpa continue.

"So Sheriff Johnson headed up the mountains to search for the outlaws. He caught up to them in a gulch known as Lowe Creek and waited until the outlaws fell asleep. He snuck up and was just about to capture the bad guys when Lonesome Bill Broom stepped out from behind a tree and pointed his guns at him. One-Eyed Jack Mahan jumped out from behind a boulder and pointed his gun, too. They tricked Sheriff Johnson by putting rocks and bushes under their blankets."

Emmy stopped walking, put her hands on her hips and asked, "So how did the sheriff capture the bad guys?"

"I'm getting to that part," Grandpa said as they turned the corner and got close to the ice cream stand. "Lonesome Bill Broom and One-Eyed Jack Mahan were ready to plug the sheriff full of lead when two shots rang out and they both fell down dead. Sheriff Johnson looked behind him and watched as Ol' Melvin and Obadiah walked out of the trees."

"Wait! I thought he was already dead. Are you saying he was a ghost and shot Lonesome Bill Broom and One-Eyed Jack Mahan?"

Grandpa shook his head while holding open the door to Robbins Old Fashioned Ice Cream Parlor. "Nope! Ol' Melvin was a tough ol' prospector and the conk on his head just knocked him out for a while. He tied a red bandana over the wound and followed the outlaws."

"And he shot both outlaws dead in the middle of the night with one eye and an old rusty rifle, huh?"

"It might have been a lucky shot," Grandpa admitted with a chuckle. "After that word spread about the gold strike and within a month over a hundred, I mean a thousand miners knew about it. Soon the town of Soldnerville was full of miners and they even started the mining camp they named Polanka Gorge. Ol' Melvin and Obadiah didn't like living in a town full of people so they moved on to another mountain and built a fancy log cabin with three rooms. They lived there for another thirty years and spent all their time diggin' for more gold. Now what would you like to order?"

"I'd like a small hot fudge sundae."

"I'm going to order a large Coke because my throat is parched after telling you about the mountains of Wyoming."

"I like your stories, Grandpa, but maybe you better stick to your day job."

"And what might that be?"

"Being the best grandpa in the whole world," Emmy said with a smile.

Grandpa laughed. "Fine! You can order the biggest sundae they have."

"Can I have whipped cream and nuts?"

"Only because I love you so much," he answered.

Part 2

—◆—

"Thanks for the ice cream, Grandpa. It was scrumptious," Emmy said as they left the ice cream shop.

"You are welcome, sweetie. That was a lot of ice cream for such a little girl," Grandpa replied.

Emmy put her hands on her hips. "Grandpa! I'm not a little girl anymore. I'm eight and will be in third grade when school starts."

After walking for a minute, Emmy asked, "Do you have another story about Ol' Melvin and Obadiah?"

"I just might," Grandpa answered with a grin.

"Okay, but without outlaws this time."

Grandpa removed his sweaty, baseball cap and ran his fingers through his wiry, gray hair. "This is a story about Ol' Melvin when he first struck gold in the Utah desert." Grandpa replaced his cap and sat down on a wooden bench facing the busy street.

Emmy hopped from one foot to the other as she faced Grandpa. "Have you ever been to Utah?"

"Once a long time ago. I took your grandmother. She didn't care much for the area, but I did. You should sit down and I'll tell you the story, okay?"

She did as he asked.

"This was when Melvin was a younger man and he and Obadiah could get around better. They had been prospecting in Colorado but then decided to head west into Utah. The traveled for several weeks up and down the mountain and hills and across mesas and desert canyons. It was tough going and they hadn't seen any signs of civilization for over a month."

"Did they see Indians?"

Grandpa shook his head. "This was in land where not even the Indians lived. There was no water or any game. Finally, they came to an overlook high on the edge of a mesa. They could see for miles in every direction. There were canyons and way off in the distance he could see a small sliver of water with a few cottonwood trees."

"I know what those are. I read about them in a book."

"Ol' Melvin looked down and could just make out a narrow trail heading down. It had to be over a thousand feet down a sheer cliff to the next level of flat land. He told Obadiah they needed to be careful and then started down the narrow path. One wrong move and they would slip over the edge and fall to their death."

"Was he scared?"

"He wasn't really scared, but he was nervous. The trail dropped down and then switched back and forth. One time they came to a place where the trail had been washed out. He stopped and looked at it. He looked back up the trail and there wasn't enough room to turn around. They had to keep going. He looked Obadiah in the eyes and said, 'We only have about a foot wide trail, but we have to keep going. I'll unload the packs and carry them across to that spot where the trail widens. Then I'll come back and you follow along.'"

"Did Obadiah understand him?"

"Yeah, because they had been together a long time," Grandpa answered. "Melvin carried all the packs across by hugging the side of the cliff. He had done the last one and came back for Obadiah, who was pawing at the trail. Just then they both heard a loud rumbling noise from above. Melvin looked up and saw an avalanche heading their way. 'Obadiah, you best hurry across.' Obadiah scooted across the gap and they made it to the wider section just as tons of rock and dirt rushed past where they had just been." Grandpa waved his arms and made a loud whooshing sound.

Emmy's eyes sparkled as she stared at Grandpa.

"For almost a minute the avalanche thundered past where Ol' Melvin and Obadiah had just stood. When it finally stopped and the dust cleared, they looked back. All signs of the trail were totally gone for over a hundred feet. 'Whew! That was sure a close one,' Melvin said and Obadiah brayed in reply. They kept heading down and made it to the creek he had seen from far above. It took three days to reach the creek. They set up camp and Melvin did some exploring. He found a spot that looked promising."

"Did he find some gold?"

"He found a few small pieces and some flecks of gold, but not enough to make much money. But he did see something else that worried him."

"What did he see?" Emmy asked as she stood up facing Grandpa.

"He saw mountain lion tracks and later that night he and Obadiah could hear the mountain lion growling in the dark. Luckily, he had his rusty, old Robnett rifle with him."

"Did he shoot the mountain lion?"

Grandpa knew Emmy didn't like to hear about any animal getting hurt, so he shook his head and said, "No, he saw the mountain lion the next morning. It was going after Obadiah, so he fired into the air and the mountain lion ran away. Melvin watched the mountain lion scamper up the rocks until it disappeared high above them. 'Well, Obadiah, I guess that critter won't harm you now and I might have found a way out of this canyon.'"

"Couldn't they go back the way they came?"

"No, because of the avalanche."

"Right! I forgot about that." Emmy sat beside Grandpa

again. "He was lucky it didn't kill him."

Grandpa rubbed his jaw for a moment and then continued. "They packed up camp and began following the trail of the mountain lion. It wound back and forth and up and down the side of the steep canyon walls. After a long day of climbing, they finally made it to the top of the other side. Melvin waited until he caught his breath and looked out across the wide canyon. 'Obadiah, I reckon we better head to more hospitable land before we get trapped for sure.' That's when he headed north and eventually ended up in Wyoming."

"And that's when he struck it rich, huh?"

Grandpa nodded. "But that was many years later. Ol' Melvin and Obadiah had many more adventures over the years before they found all the gold in Polanka Creek."

Emmy stood up and took Grandpa's hand. "We better get back before it storms. We don't want to get caught in a flash flood or an avalanche."

Grandpa laughed and stood up. "We wouldn't want that to happen."

"You will have to tell me more stories about Ol' Melvin and Obadiah before school starts."

"I hope I can remember all the stories. My memory isn't what it used to be."

Emmy smiled.

Part 3

—◆—

"Mom! Can I ride Diane's bike to see Grandpa and Grandma? I promised I would help Grandpa paint their old porch swing," Emmy hollered as she dashed up the back steps and into the kitchen. "Can I go?"

Mom wiped her hands on a dish towel and sighed. "I am making lasagna for dinner. Will you be back in time to eat?"

Emmy grinned, smacked her lips and rubbed her hands together. "I'll make sure we finish in time. I love homemade lasagna."

Emmy borrowed her older sister's dilapidated bike and raced along the sidewalks to her grandparents' house. She nearly wiped out on the loose gravel behind their house but managed to stay upright. She arrived and jumped off the bike and let it fall to the ground. "Grandpa, I'm here to help," she hollered. She dashed to the back of the house where Grandpa was working on the old porch swing.

"I'm glad you made it. I just finished getting this thing ready for a new coat of paint," Grandpa said.

"What color did Grandma choose?"

Grandpa opened the can of paint and stirred it.

"I like red," Emmy said grabbing one of the brushes.

Emmy and Grandpa worked for almost an hour adding the new coat of red paint. Grandma brought out some iced tea and Emmy and Grandpa sat on the porch steps to take a break.

"Can you tell me another story while we wait for the paint to dry?" Emmy asked.

Grandpa chuckled and said, "I guess that would be better than watching the paint dry."

"Tell me more about Ol' Melvin and Obadiah. Did they have more adventures?"

Grandpa wiped some paint off of his arm and then wiped a few specks from Emmy's cheek. "I think I remember a story about the time Ol' Melvin and Obadiah had wandered close to the Grand Canyon."

"I saw pictures of the Grand Canyon at the library. I want to go there someday. Have you ever seen it?" Emmy asked.

"We were at the South Rim once, but this story is about the other side. It was getting close to winter and Ol' Melvin and Obadiah decided to head south for warmer weather. They had been travelin' for several days through a forest of different types of pine trees and shrubs. It was hard going because of the dense forest and they could only see a few feet in front of them." Grandpa smacked at a fly but missed. "It was about noon this one day and they had been travelin' since sunrise. Melvin ducked under a big pine tree and came to a sudden stop. He froze in place and was afraid to move for fear of losing his balance."

"What happened? Did he see a bear or a mountain lion like before?"

Grandpa shook his head. "No, Emmy, he stopped because if he had taken another step he would have fallen down a thousand foot cliff!"

Emmy's eyes opened wide. "Was it the Grand Canyon?"

"It was, but Ol' Melvin and Obadiah didn't know it at the time. You see this was before anyone except the local native people even knew there was a Grand Canyon. Anyway,

Melvin grabbed hold of Obadiah's rein before he lost his footing. He and Obadiah stood on the edge and looked out at the canyon. He shook his head and said, 'Wow, Obadiah, that sure is a big ditch to cross.' Both of them stared at the huge canyon."

Emmy held her hands out as far as she could. "I think its wider than the Kinmundy River valley."

"Much wider. It's so wide that Ol' Melvin and Obadiah could barely see the other rim which was over ten miles away. Melvin looked at Obadiah and said, 'I reckon we need to find a way down if we want to keep heading to warmer weather.' They made camp, ate lunch and then explored the area for several days. Melvin caught some rabbits to eat..."

"Oh, why did he have to eat bunnies?"

Grandpa clenched his jaw, then explained, "These weren't soft little bunnies like you see today. These were wild, desert rabbits that people caught to make stew out of."

"That's okay then. Did he put carrots and potatoes in the stew?"

"He didn't have any potatoes, but he had a few carrots left and he found different kinds of roots to use."

Emmy made a face. "That sounds gross. I wouldn't want to eat roots."

"Back then the old prospectors had to eat whatever they could find. Melvin added salt and pepper to make the stew taste better. After exploring for a few days, Melvin found a narrow trail heading down the canyon."

"Was it like the one you told me about before?"

"In some ways, but this trail was wider and wound all around as it went down. Deeper and deeper they followed the switchbacks down the trail. Ol' Melvin and Obadiah went lower and lower into the canyon until they couldn't see the top. Finally, they came to a mighty river. It's called the Colorado now, but it didn't have a name back then. They set up camp at the edge of the river while they tried to figure out a way to get across. They ended up staying there for the whole winter. They built a shelter out of rocks and old logs and survived on wild plants, desert rabbits and other creatures."

"Did they eat rattlesnakes?"

Grandpa nodded.

"I don't mind if they ate those. I wouldn't eat one, but it's okay Ol' Melvin and Obadiah did."

"Then Melvin had an idea. He would build a raft and they would go down the river until they found a place to climb out. All winter Melvin worked on his canoe. He had to make it big enough to carry Obadiah and all their supplies."

"Couldn't they swim down the river? Can't donkeys swim?"

"No, the river was much too wild. There were rapids and he didn't know if there was a big waterfall just around the bend. So, they survived the winter. He even found a little bit of gold and silver to take with them. One day he said to Obadiah, 'I reckon it's time to move on.' He loaded up the boat and helped Obadiah get in and off they went." Grandpa stood up, waved his arms and moved back and forth like he was careening down a wild river. "The river went this way and that." Grandpa moved back and forth and up and down like he was going around the bends of the river. "They went down the whitewater rapids on the flimsy raft while Melvin kept his eyes peeled for danger. That went on for three whole days before they came to a spot where the river settled down and they could get to the bank. They found a sandy beach and made camp."

Grandma opened the back door and stood with hands on hips. "Are you going to keep flapping your tongue all day, or are you going to finish painting my swing. I do want to use it again this summer."

"I suppose I will have to finish the story later, Emmy. We better do what Grandma says."

"I know they made it down the river, Grandpa, because you told me they lived for almost a hundred years." Emmy touched the paint. "It's dry enough for another coat. I want to hear how Ol' Melvin and Obadiah made it out of the canyon."

"You're right. They did make it out, but they had lots of adventures before they did." Grandpa grinned and said, "They even had to escape a herd of wild horses."

"I want to hear about that," she said and then looked up at Grandpa. "You know it's truly amazing that Obadiah never fell out of the canoe or the boat or the raft," Emmy said as she dipped her brush into the paint.

Grandpa chuckled and replied, "Yes, he must have been quite an agile donkey."

Part 4

—◆—

Several days later Emmy rode the bicycle to her grandparents' house again. She saw them sitting on the newly painted swing and rode the bike all the way to the porch before jumping off.

"My word, Emily, you must not jump off that bicycle so fast. You will hurt yourself," Grandma Mary Colasanti said.

Emmy shrugged and said, "I do it all the time, Grandma. I never get hurt."

"Did your father fix the leak under the kitchen sink?" Grandpa asked.

Emmy nodded as she dashed up the steps and sat between her grandparents. "He fixed that and the toilet because it wouldn't flush right and he even did something with the electricity in the basement."

"Good. He's got plenty of projects to do before he tries to sell that house."

Grandma stopped the swing and turned to look at her husband. "I didn't know he was going to sell the house. Why didn't anyone tell me?"

"He wants to fix it up and buy a bigger place. Don't know if he ever will though," Grandpa answered. He patted Emmy's leg. "I suppose you want to hear more about Ol' Melvin and Obadiah."

Emmy grinned and leaned close to him. "Unless you have another story about Perkins MacGhee. I like those stories, too."

Grandma stood up. "While you are filling this child's head with more of your fanciful, tall tales, I am going to make lunch. I have some leftover lasagna. Would you like some, Emily?"

Emmy rubbed her belly. "You know I love leftover lasagna. Mom made some the day we painted the swing. I ate more the next day than I did the first night."

Grandma went inside and Grandpa and Emmy began rocking in the humid August air.

"You said Ol' Melvin and Obadiah had to escape a herd of wild horses but didn't tell me how."

Grandpa watched two squirrels chasing each other around one of the trees and thought for a moment. "Yes, I remember it now. Melvin and Obadiah were in the river canyon doing some exploring when they saw a cloud of dust over the horizon. They stopped and in a few seconds they heard a terrible racket."

"Did it sound like a herd of wild horses?" Emmy asked with a giggle.

"I'm sure it did," Grandpa said pulling on her ponytail. "Within seconds they could see the stampeding horses coming straight at them. Melvin looked around and saw a group of boulders at the edge of a creek. 'Obadiah,' he said. 'I reckon our only chance to escape is to squeeze in between those boulders.' So he jerked on Obadiah's rein and pulled him to safety just in the nick of time."

"He did that a lot didn't he, Grandpa?"

"Yes, that's how they survived to be so old," Grandpa answered. "After they escaped the wild horses, they kept heading west and then south as they explored more of the giant canyon. They found a tributary and followed it until they came to an impassable waterfall. There was a large pool at the base of the waterfall, so Ol' Melvin jumped in and took a bath. 'Obadiah,' he hollered. 'I ain't had a good bath in four or five years. You should get in and get rid of some of the dust.' So, Obadiah stuck one leg in the water to test it. Then he got into the pool and took a bath along with Ol' Melvin."

"That would have been so funny to see," Emmy said as she giggled.

Grandpa laughed. "It would have been a sight to see. A man and a donkey scrubbing off the dirt in a pool of water."

"He must have been pretty stinky. Sometimes Daddy comes home from work and Mommy makes him take a bath before she let's him kiss her."

"I can understand that. Your grandmother has made me take a shower before she even lets me in the house," Grandpa said. "Back in the old times people out west didn't have bathtubs like we do today. They would have to go to a saloon or a hotel and pay money to take a bath and the water was usually cold."

"What else happened to Ol' Melvin and Obadiah? Anything special?"

"Melvin decided to go back up the river when it started getting too hot. He would prospect for gold and silver along the way but didn't find much. He did come across some friendly Indians and stayed with them for a while. The Indians gave him some food in exchange for some new blankets."

"I was wondering if he and Obadiah ever ate anything."

"They traveled back up the canyon until they found an old cattle trail heading up the south side. It took a couple days, and Obadiah nearly fell over the side one time, but they finally made it to the top of the canyon. Melvin took off his old cap, shook out some of the dust and looked out over the wide canyon. He shook his head and said to Obadiah, 'I don't know if this place has a name, but it sure is a grand canyon.' And Obadiah made a noise that sounded like a donkey's laugh." Grandpa laughed and then said, "He haw. He haw," over and over.

"Oh, Grandpa." Emmy nudged his side. "You're silly. He didn't really name the Grand Canyon, did he?"

"Maybe, maybe not, but he was one of the first men to explore it. After leaving the canyon, Ol' Melvin and Obadiah headed south. They came to more mountains and lots of red desert. Today the place is called Sedona, Arizona. Lots of people go there because they think it's a special place with magical powers."

"Special how?"

"Some people believe there's an unexplained force that goes through the area that gives off energy."

"Does it really?"

Grandpa shrugged. "I don't know, but while Ol' Melvin and Obadiah were there they were attacked by hostile Indians. They were almost trapped again. They were forced to climb a small mountain shaped like a huge bell while the Indians rode all around it and made loud noises while shooting arrows at them. Then some of the Indians jumped off their horses and started climbing up after them. Ol' Melvin and Obadiah kept climbing higher and higher until they were at the very top of the bell-shaped mountain."

"How did they get away?" Emmy asked. "You better not tell me they flew off the mountain in a balloon. I wouldn't believe that for a second."

Grandpa shook his head. "They were standing at the very top of the mountain when all of a sudden they heard a buzzing sound coming from inside it. The Indians heard it too and they stopped in their tracks. The mountain began to vibrate gently as the noise got louder. The vibrations grew stronger and stronger and Ol' Melvin and Obadiah were nearly knocked off their feet. The Indians had heard the sound before and thought it was their ancestors warning them to stay off the mountain. So the Indians raced down the mountain, got on their horses and rode away. After that Ol' Melvin and Obadiah never had anymore trouble with Indians. The legend among the Indians was told over and over about Ol' Melvin and Obadiah and how they were able to command their ancestors inside the mountain. That's why Melvin and Obadiah were able to travel all over without any fear from the natives."

"I'm glad the Indians didn't shoot them and they became friends," Emmy said. "I can smell lasagna so I think we better go inside before Grandma eats it all."

"Good idea, Emmy. She loves lasagna almost as much as you."

They went inside and finished the lasagna and a garden salad Grandma put together. Then they went outside to let their food digest.

"That was so good. My belly is full," Emmy said as she rubbed her stomach.

"It was at that, Emmy. I shouldn't have eaten so much, but I couldn't help having a second plate."

"Did that mountain really vibrate?"

"It did and Melvin and Obadiah almost lost their footing. They came real close to slipping down the mountain."

"That would not have been very good," Emmy said. "The unfriendly Indians would have captured them."

"After the Indians left, Melvin and Obadiah climbed down, and they made camp that night beside a small creek. They ate the last of their root stew and in the morning he was washing out his iron kettle in the stream when he spotted something shiny in the water."

"Was it more gold?"

"It was enough gold for them to buy enough supplies to last for another whole year. Since he had such good luck there, he gave the creek a special name."

"What did he call it?"

Grandpa rubbed his jaw for a moment and then grinned. "He decided to call it the Good Fortune Creek, and it's still there to this very day. Now lots of people pan for gold there, but none of them have ever found any."

"Why not?"

"It's because the spirits in the mountain hid all the gold from anyone who hadn't climbed to the top."

Part 5

—◆—

Joseph Colasanti waved as his daughter-in-law drove away. He smiled as his younger granddaughter raced up the sidewalk. "Why aren't you in school, Emmy?"

"Grandpa! Today's Saturday, and school doesn't start till next week. Mom dropped me off because she got called into work and didn't want to leave me home with Diane." Emmy Colasanti watched her grandfather planting bulbs in the front flower bed. "What are those called?"

"Your grandmother called them Ruby Giants and these are Red Hats. "

"Will they grow into giant flowers?" Emmy asked raising her hands high over her head.

Grandpa laughed and answered, "I don't think so. That's the last one. I need a break."

He sat on the front porch steps and Emmy snuggled close.

He looked at her and smiled. "From your expression I can tell you want something."

"Can you tell me another story?"

"Ol' Melvin and Obadiah or Perkins MacGhee?"

"Either one, but I like the ones about Melvin better."

Grandpa waved as the neighbor across the street finished mowing his yard. "Another one about Ol' Melvin, huh?" Grandpa rubbed his chin.

"You need a shave, Grandpa. Does Grandma let you kiss her with that scruffy beard?"

"Sometimes. How about this one? It happened in the

mountains and plateaus of Utah after they escaped the Indians in Sedona."

"I remember that story," Emmy said.

"Ol' Melvin and Obadiah had been traveling for many weeks and it was getting close to winter. They only had enough provisions to last one more week at most."

"Did they mostly eat beans and biscuits?"

"Sometimes they had bacon and once in a while he would trap rabbits."

"He shouldn't kill bunnies."

"Sometimes he had to so they wouldn't starve."

"Okay," she said. "But they shouldn't kill them too often."

"They were in this place where there were lots of funny shaped rocks sticking up from the ground. He said to Obadiah, 'Those looks like people sticking out of the ground.' Obadiah looked over the edge at the funny hoodoos..."

"The what?"

"People call them hoodoos now because of the funny shape."

"Are you talking about a real place?"

"Yes, and people visit there every day. So, they were running out of food and didn't have any gold to buy anything. They decided to go down one of the trails and see if they could find some gold and silver. They headed down and wound all around these strange formations. Obadiah heard a rattler. Melvin saw it and killed it, and they ate that for dinner. They were setting up camp when they heard someone coming up the trail."

"Was it more Indians?"

Grandpa shook his head. "No! It was another old prospector they knew from New Mexico. His name was Walker Andrews and he had an old donkey he called Python."

Emmy laughed. "Why would he call his donkey

Python? That's a kind of snake."

"He couldn't think of a better name, I guess. He didn't know any better. Anyway, he saw Melvin and Obadiah and shouted 'It's good to see you again. I broke my ol' Cray saddlebag and this dang NEC rifle is busted. I dropped it last week on Oracle Mountain.'"

"He must not have been a very good prospector," Emmy said.

"He struggled with his gear. Anyway, Melvin said 'Let me take a look later. You're always breaking your stuff and I have to fix it. Do you have anything to eat?' Then Andrews said, 'All I've got left is this Apple. You can have it if you want.'"

"A real apple?" Emmy asked.

"Yes, Andrews had been in this valley in California where they grew Macintosh apples. He offered it to Obadiah and he ate the whole thing."

"Even the seeds?"

"Every bit including the core. So, then Melvin and Walker started a campfire and they told stories about where they had been prospecting until late into the night. Melvin talked about the mountain shaped like a bell and how the Olidata Indians almost captured him. Then Andrews told Melvin about the time he had been prospecting in the Meebox River up in Montana territory and found a nugget as big as his fist."

"Did he really find one that big?"

"He was probably making it up, but he might have found one as big as a kernal." Grandpa slapped his arm. "Those pesky bugs are biting me again."

"You should use something to prevent the bugs from attacking you."

"So they talked until the sun came up and Andrews checked his Cray saddlebag and guess what he found."

"What?"

"He found an old cookie and split it with Ol' Melvin. Then they heard a loud noise and something pinged off the rocks behind them."

"Was it more Indians?"

"No, it was bandits from Java, Colorado. They were wanted for robbing banks if my memory serves me right."

"Did the bank robbers know they were there?"

"No, they were trying to escape a posse. The kept riding and Melvin, Obadiah, Andrews and Python had another close call. Then Melvin fixed Walker's gear and he found a can of Spam in the bottom of the saddlebag."

"Grandpa!" Emmy said standing up and putting her hands on her hips. "They didn't have Spam back in the old days, did they?"

Grandpa nodded. "Emmy, spam has always been around."

Part 6

—◆—

"Grandpa, can you help me with my homework, please?" Emmy asked. "I don't understand this question."

Grandpa read the question and rubbed his jaw. "I'm not sure what it means, either. Maybe you should ask your Grandma when she gets back from the store."

"Okay, but since I can't finish my homework, could you tell me another Melvin and Obadiah story?"

"I suppose I could, but let's make some popcorn first."

"I like popcorn especially if it has lots of butter on it."

Grandpa put the popcorn in the microwave, and Emmy watched the bag grow bigger and bigger. Then Grandpa poured it into two bowls. They sat on the back porch swing to eat.

"This is a story about how Ol' Melvin met Obadiah when they were both real young."

"Where did they meet?" Emmy asked with a handful of the buttery popcorn.

"They met in the mountains of West Texas. It was long before the Civil War and in fact Texas was still part of Mexico."

"Was it really?" Emmy asked wiping her hand on her pants.

"It was, but not for much longer. You see Melvin was part of General Sam Houston's secret army. He would prospect for gold and at the same time, he would keep track of Santa Anna's Mexican army."

"Was that a girl general?"

"No, but it sounds like it, huh? Anyway, one day Melvin was following the army, and he got too reckless. He was watching them from the top of this ridge of rocks and small boulders. He moved to get a better look and some of the rocks slid down the hill. The Mexican soldiers heard the small avalanche and rushed up the hill."

"Did they capture Ol' Melvin?"

"No! They thought they would, but before they could climb the hill, he raced down the other side and jumped into a gully. He ran for over two miles down first one gully then another. He ran harder than he ever had. He ended up in a place called the Sonora Wash. There was just a trickle of water at the bottom because it was so hot and hadn't rained for several months. Melvin was so thirsty he got down and scooped up the water in his hands and drank it even though it was full of sand. He was so busy drinking the water he didn't notice a mountain lion sneaking up behind him." Grandpa moved his hands like he was trying to sneak up on Emmy. "Closer and closer the mountain came."

"Oh, no. Poor Melvin." Emmy put her hands to her face and sighed.

"Just before the mountain lion was going to attack, a wild donkey came rushing across the stream and kicked the mountain lion. It ran off and Melvin was saved. He was so grateful that he gave the donkey the last of his biscuits and some oats he had in his backpack. The donkey ate the food and then started following Melvin around. After about a month Melvin figured the donkey was going to stay, so he made camp one night, shared some rabbit... I mean turtle..."

Emmy made a face.

"No, it was a wild turkey and it was around Thanksgiving Day. Melvin decided he had better give the donkey a name. So he said, 'You've been following me everywhere for over a month now, I reckon it's time I give you a name.' He scratched his ear and then scratched the donkey's ear. 'I don't know what most people call their donkeys, but how would you like to be called Obadiah? When I was a young boy, my mama tool me to Sunday School and she read the Bible to me. She made me memorize the names of all the books, and I really liked the name Obadiah. So I reckon since you saved my skin back there at Sonora Wash, I'm gonna call you Obadiah.'"

"Did the donkey like that name?" Emmy scooped up the last of her popcorn and ate it.

"He sure did! He nodded his head and made a braying sound like a donkey laughing. After that Ol' Melvin and Obadiah were inseparable. Melvin bought special saddlebags that fit over Obadiah's back, and Obadiah learned how to carry all their gear. They traveled all over Texas, New Mexico, Arizona and every state out there prospecting for gold. Every once in a while, Obadiah would wander off and Melvin would find him near a small creek. Obadiah would bray and nod his head and Melvin would do some panning in the creek, and do you know what?"

"What, Grandpa?"

"Almost every time Melvin would find enough gold to buy more provisions to keep wandering all over the territories. They traveled from Mexico way up north to Canada and met a lot of other prospectors and donkey, but he never met another donkey as smart as Obadiah."

Part 7

—◆—

"Grandpa, didn't Ol' Melvin ever get super lonely prospecting in the hill and mountains all by himself?" Emmy asked one afternoon as she and Grandpa were taking a walk around the block.

"Well, I suppose he must have sometimes. But he did go into towns every now and again to buy supplies. He probably spent a little time in the saloons sipping whiskey like all the other prospectors and miners did. They didn't have TVs or radios like we do now."

"I get bored if I can't play with my friends."

"Most people like to be around other people but there are some who like it better if they never see anyone else. I guess Ol' Melvin was one of them fellers," Grandpa said with a chuckle. "That reminds me of a time when he kinda struck it rich for a while. He decided to head into town to buy new clothes and boots."

"Did he need new underwear?" she asked and then giggled.

Grandpa laughed and answered, "Back then he wore what we call long johns. They were almost like another pair of britches under his outer pants. He was in the mountains somewhere in Colorado. He mined enough gold to take to town. First he made sure no one could find his claim then he and Obadiah headed down the mountain to the boomtown of Silver Gulch. It was a rowdy town full of miners, gamblers and plain old outlaws. There was a saloon on every corner and no sheriff or deputy to maintain law and order."

"Why did he go there? Couldn't he go to the next town?"

"It wasn't like here where it's easy to go from SoHam to New Linden or Crest Ridge. Silver Gulch was the only town around for miles and miles. If he needed supplies, he had to go there. Now Melvin always kept a rifle with him for protection against wild animals, so he wasn't afraid to go into Silver Gulch. Even with only one eye, he could hit a running rabbit at fifty yards."

Emmy put a hand to her mouth. "I forgot he only had one good eye."

"To tell the truth, I kinda forgot, too," Grandpa admitted. "So, he went down the mountain into town and the first thing he saw was two men fighting in the street. Then he heard gunshots at the other end of the street, and one man fell down dead. Then more people flew out of another saloon door and started punching each other. One of them cracked the other over the head with a bottle. He turned around just as three riders galloped down the main street shooting their guns into the air. He looked at Obadiah and said, 'There are too many people in this town. I like peace and quiet to fall asleep, but I don't think we're gonna get any in Silver Gulch. We might have to buy our supplies and head out of town before sundown.' Obadiah didn't like the noise either."

Emmy covered her ears. "I wouldn't like it. I don't like hearing gunshots."

"Yeah, we do hear some of those from the neighborhood across Washington Boulevard, huh?"

Emmy nodded.

"Melvin tied Obadiah to the hitching post outside the general store. He checked the street to see if anyone was watching, but they weren't. He went inside and put his bag of gold on the counter. The man who ran the store used some scales to see how much the bag was worth. He told Melvin,

70

and Melvin told the man what he needed. The man said it would take an hour, so Melvin went outside. He whispered to Obadiah, 'I reckon one sip of whiskey won't hurt me none. My throat is mighty parched. You stay here and wait for the supplies.' Obadiah brayed to show he understood. Melvin looked up and down the street. There were so many saloons to choose from. He saw one called The King of Hearts, so he decided to try it. He headed inside and the place was empty except for the bartender with slicked back hair, two men who looked like gunslingers with pistols strapped to their legs and a man in a black suit with a waxed mustache. Melvin ordered a whiskey and the man in the suit wandered over and said, 'I ain't ever seen you in Silver Gulch before. What's your name? I'm known as Black Bill and this is my saloon. Would you like to join me and my friends in a friendly game of cards?' Melvin knew a crooked game when he saw one, but he grinned, swallowed the whiskey and said, 'I ain't much good at cards, but as long as it's a friendly game, I have time to waste.' He followed Black Bill to the table and sat down. He tossed a silver dollar on the table and asked, 'Will that get me in the game?' The other men who looked like they were falling asleep, suddenly came to life."

"Why did he do that, Grandpa? Didn't he worry about losing all his money?"

"Ah! Let me finish the story. For a few hands Ol' Melvin deliberately lost the bets. The other men grinned and encouraged him to bet even more. Melvin shook his head and said, 'I don't know. Maybe one or two more hands, but I ain't never been any good at poker. I have troubled remembering which card make good hands.' The other men couldn't believe their good fortune. The next hand they ran up the pot until Melvin didn't have anything left. Much to their surprise, he won the pot. After he won the next five hands, they were ready to kill him. He decided it was time to leave, so he walked out. Just before he got to the door, he flipped the bartender a silver dollar and said, 'Buy them all a drink on Ol' Melvin Boyd.' Black Bill and his gunslingers stared at each other."

"Why?"

"Well, you see Ol' Melvin had a reputation for being a slick gambler. He used his appearance as an old prospector to his advantage. Every few years he would find himself in a town much like Silver Gulch, and he always walked away with more money than he started with."

Emmy shrugged.

"By now the man at the general store had all the supplies packed into Obadiah's saddle bags. Melvin paid him and headed out of town. About a mile back up the mountain, the two gunslingers stepped out from behind a large boulder. They were wearing masks, but Melvin recognized them by their smell. 'Hand over all our money!' they said while pointing their guns at Melvin. Now Ol' Melvin knew he was likely to get ambushed, so he had sent Obadiah on ahead. The gunslingers weren't in position early enough to see Obadiah go by. Melvin shook like he was scared to death and said, 'You can have all the money if you don' kill me.' He said that last part much louder. When he heard Ol' Melvin raise his voice, Obadiah charged out from his hiding place and kicked them gunslingers in the head. They fell down as if dead. Ol' Melvin laughed as he took their guns. 'Obadiah, I reckon this is why I hate going into town so much. And the worst part is I forgot to buy new boots.'"

Part 8

—◆—

"Thanks for helping me with my homework, Grandma. Grandpa couldn't figure it out," Emmy said. She walked out the front door and saw Grandpa sitting on the steps.

"Did your grandmother help you?"

"She did. It's all done now."

Grandpa put an arm around her as she sat next to him. I thought of another story about Ol' Melvin and Obadiah. Do you want to hear it?"

"Sure, I have to wait until Daddy can pick me up."

"This one takes place a few years later than the last one. Ol' Melvin, Obadiah, Walker Andrews and Python were heading north in the spring. They wanted to see the land called Canada because they had heard their was gold just laying in the creeks waiting for someone to come along and scoop it up. They loaded up their provisions and headed from Colorado through Wyoming and up into Montana Territory. They wandered back and forth along the mountains. Sometimes they would stop and prospect for gold in Montana and others times they would be in Idaho."

"That's where potatoes come from," Emmy said.

"They grow a lot of potatoes there, sweetie. Ol' Melvin saw a bunch of different animals. He saw sheep with big horns that wrapped in a circle. He saw some bears and even a few wolves, but the wolves mostly stayed away. He could hear them at night when the stars were out. One night he tried to count all the stars, but since he didn't know any numbers bigger than a hundred, he had to stop. He said to Walker

Andrews, 'I reckon there must be near a thousand stars in the sky up here in Montana.' Andrews looked up and said, 'It looks like the sky goes on forever.' They kept moving north and to the west. They made their way into Canada and followed rivers and had to cross giant mountain passes that were still covered in snow at the top. They even saw a glacier that stretched as far as they could see up a valley. They didn't find any gold though. So they kept traveling to the west. They finally arrived in what we now call Alaska. The only people they saw were natives who built houses out of snow and ice. They couldn't understand them, but they traded things like pelts and food. Ol' Melvin even had a bottle of whiskey. He traded it for some whale oil."

"Why did he have whiskey, Grandpa?"

"He needed it in case of snakebite or if he got real sick. It was like medicine."

Emmy didn't really believe it, but she didn't say anything.

"The natives told them about a land farther north where the tallest mountain in the world rose up higher than anyone could see right out of the flat plain. Ol' Melvin and Walker Andrews thought there might be gold up there. So they headed north. It took months and they had to build a shelter to survive the winter, but when it was spring again, they started traveling. Finally, they got to a hill and out in the distance they saw the mountain the natives called Denali."

"Is that a real mountain?"

"Yes, and I could show you a picture later. Your grandmother and I were in Alaska one year and we saw it. So, Melvin, Obadiah, Andrews and Python headed for the mountain. It took them weeks to get there even though it looked like it was just a mile away."

"Did they climb it?"

"They tried, but there was too much snow and it was

74

too steep. They looked for gold, but didn't find any. There was enough deer and elk and other game to keep them from starving. They decided to go south before they got caught in another winter. For months they traveled south. Up and over mountains. Across wide rivers and through wide meadows and valleys. After what seemed to take forever, they stood on top of the last mountain. They gazed out at a body of water in front of them that went on farther than they could see. In between that mountain and the one east of them was a wide valley filled with a glacier. They made their way down the mountain and got to the glacier. They walked all the way to the edge and stared down at the water a hundred feet below. Than all at once there was a mighty roar. Louder than a dozen jet airplanes taking off at the same time."

"What was it, Grandpa?" Emmy asked.

"The glacier began to shake and before they knew it, a giant chunk of the ice broke off and carried Ol' Melvin and Obadiah with it. He could see Walker Andrews and Python still standing at the top of the glacier as they held onto the ice for dear life."

"It's a good thing Obadiah was an agile donkey, huh, Grandpa?"

"Yes, it was. Well, the next thing Melvin knew, he and Obadiah were on top of this iceberg. They could see Andrews and Python, so they waved goodbye. 'Well, Obadiah,' Melvin said. 'I reckon we're gonna go for a ride. Good thing we still have our food.' They hunkered down and rode that iceberg south and east. They went past Alaska and part of Canada and then more of Alaska. They were just far enough away from the coast they couldn't swim to land. They went past too many islands to count. They made it past the biggest island and were then off the coast of what is now Washington. The ocean current kept them just close enough to the coast to let them see the land, but not close enough to reach it."

"Too bad they couldn't build a canoe made out of ice," Emmy said.

"They tried that but it melted in the sun. They were drifting south all the time. They sailed down the coast past Washington and then Oregon. When they got to Northern California, they could see trees that must have been five hundred feet tall as straight as an arrow. Now the water was getting warmer and their once huge iceberg was getting smaller and smaller. Melvin knew it would soon melt away and they would have to swim for it."

"Did it melt into a small ice cube?" Emmy asked with a grin.

"It melted enough that there wasn't room for them to stand on it anymore. 'Well, Obadiah, I reckon we are gonna get out feet wet.' They were ready to jump into the ocean when they heard someone shouting."

"Who was it?"

"Ol' Melvin put his hand up to his eyes to shield them from the sun. He laughed and slapped Obadiah on the rump. 'Well I'll be a monkey's uncle. Look over yonder, Obadiah. That's Walker Andrews and some natives heading this way in three canoes. Maybe we won't drown after all.' That's how Walker Andrews rescued Ol' Melvin and Obadiah. They made it to shore and then discovered gold in California."

"Did they become rich?"

"They made enough money to buy whatever they wanted. Ol' Melvin tried living in a big city for a few months, but he couldn't get used to it. He decided to go back to being a prospector."

"What happened to Walker Andrews?"

"He became one of the richest men in all of California. When he was a lot older, he invented a machine to count money and made even more of a fortune. He and Python lived in a big mansion in San Francisco for a time. Then he moved to San Diego and started building ships for the Navy. Python eventually got too old and passed away. Andrews bought a plot of land in the mountains and buried him there. Andrews himself lived to be ninety-six, and after he died, they named a city after him, except they switched his name around. They named the city Andrew Walker Grove and it's still there out in California to this very day."

"Have you ever been there, Grandpa?"

"I was there many years ago. It's a nice town. Lots of palm trees and golf courses now, but I bet Ol' Melvin wouldn't like it. Too many people."

"What ever happened to Ol' Melvin and Obadiah?"

Grandpa smiled, squeezed her shoulders and answered, "That, my child, I will have to save for another time." He pointed to the street. "Your father's here, and it's time for you to go home."

She gave Grandpa a kiss, skipped down the sidewalk, turned, waved and hollered, "Thanks for all the stories, Grandpa. I love hearing them."

Tex Miller, The Last Of The Singing Cowboys

Blue Lightning

—◆—

"I want to say howdy to all my podners and all the little buckaroos who came out to see me today. I am Tex Miller, the last of the singing cowboys, and this is my horse Blue Lightning."

Tex hopped off his horse and faced the crowd of mostly young boys and girls in the town of Willis Creel, Oklahoma.

"Blue Lightning is not an ordinary horse, boys and girls. He is the smartest horse ever to ride through the fine new state of Oklahoma. Let me show you... rather... let Blue Lightning show you some of the things he knows. Let's start off with some simple 'rithmetic. I'm sure all you young cowboys and cowgirls are studying the three Rs. 'Rithmetic, reading and 'riting. Let's see if Blue can answer this."

He turned and stood next to his horse.

"Blue, do you know how many apples I would have if I went to the orchard and picked up three red apples then I went to another orchard and picked up two yellow apples? How many apples would I have all together if I didn't eat any of them?"

The crowd watched as Blue Lightning tilted his head back and forth like he was thinking. Then he snorted and pawed the ground five times.

"That's absolutely right, Blue. I think you deserve a treat, and I just happen to have an apple here somewhere."

He removed his ten-gallon Stetson hat, held up a shiny red apple and offered it to Blue Lightning. Blue took a look at the apple and shook his head hard enough that his long mane flipped back and forth.

"What? Don't you like red apples? Well, then how about a shiny yellow one!"

He pulled a second apple from his hat and Blue whinnied and ate that one.

"I guess we know what kind of apple Blue prefers."

He waited until the applause and laughter ended.

"Now for another trick."

He whispered into Blue's ear and Blue moved his head up and down. Then he backed up a few feet.

"Boys and girls, Blue is going to show you how he treats outlaws and bandits when he captures them."

With a hand signal Blue rose up on his hind legs and began pawing the air like he was boxing. The crowd roared with laughter.

"That's Blue giving the outlaws a left jab and then a right hook."

Blue dropped to all four legs and took a bow.

"He just showed you how brave he can be, but now he is going to show you how a tiny little field mouse can frighten him. Do you think a tiny field mouse can frighten Blue Lightning?"

The boys and girls shouted, "No!"

"Let's see. Blue, close your eyes for a second."

Tex made sure Blue's eyes were closed then he reached into the pocket of his fancy cowboy shirt and pulled out a white mouse.

"This is my pet mouse Mitch. I'm going to set him on the ground in front of Blue and let's see what happens."

He set the mouse down.

"Okay, Blue. Open your eyes!"

Blue opened his eyes, looked around, snorted, then he glanced at the ground in front of him. All at once, he began

81

prancing in reverse as he tried to escape the tiny creature.

"Now, Blue, it's all right. This is just my pet mouse Mitch and he won't harm you."

Tex picked up the mouse and put him back in his pocket.

"I hope you've enjoyed seeing how smart Blue Lightning is, but now it's time for me to mosey on down the road, but before I do, does anyone want to hear a cowboy song?"

The children whooped and hollered until Tex raised a hand.

"I have just enough time for two songs. Maybe three if you clap loud enough."

He reached behind his saddle, felt around and grabbed his guitar.

"I'm going to sing a song I wrote when I was twelve years old. I call it 'The Cowboy's Best Friend' and it goes like this."

Tex sang that one and then three songs since the boys and girls begged for more. He put his guitar back and got back in the saddle. He took off his cowboy hat and waved to the crowd.

"It's been mighty fine being here today. I hope you enjoyed seeing how smart Blue Lightning is, and thank you kindly for listening to my songs. Mitch thanks Blue for not stomping on him."

That drew more laughter from the crowd and Tex smiled.

"Now I want to remind all you young cowboys and cowgirls to mind your manners, listen to your Ma and Pa, don't swear or cuss and try to be good to widows and orphans."

He waved his hat as Blue Lightning reared up and pawed the air to say goodbye.

"I'm Tex Miller, the last of the singing cowboys, and maybe I'll be back to Willis Creel real soon."

He turned his horse and pranced away. The crowd could hear him singing as he rode out of town.

"I'm the last of the singing cowboys. Singin' songs of inspiration and joy."

My First Guitar

—◆—

"Howdy, podners and buckaroos. I'm Tex Miller..."

He got down from his horse and introduced Blue Lightning.

"I'm sure glad to be here today in Healy City. Me and Blue have been traveling all through your fine state of Kansas for a while now, and Blue has been showing off his tricks. Would you like to see Blue perform?"

The boys and girls shouted loud enough so Blue did some of his tricks.

"Now I want to tell you a story about my first guitar."

He grabbed a guitar from behind the saddle.

"It wasn't this one, but it was like it. Let me tell you all about it. My Ma and Pa lived on a small ranch in California. They grew all the food we needed and I helped weed the garden whenever they asked me to. You young cowboys and cowgirls need to help out on the ranch and farm whenever you can. Now we didn't have much money, but I saw this man playing a guitar one day when we went into town for supplies. I stood in front of him and listened as he played it and sang songs. He let me hold his guitar and showed me where to put my fingers to make chords. I was enchanted by this guitar, so on the way back to the ranch, I told Ma and Pa that all I wanted for my next birthday, or the next Christmas, whichever came first, was a guitar. I had to wait for a long time it seemed, but when Christmas came around, there was a guitar under the little scrub pine tree we had decorated. I thanked Ma and Pa and promised to practice every day and still do my chores. I learned how to play my guitar and carried it with me everywhere. When I was a bit older, I wrote some songs."

He played one of the songs.

"Now I'll tell you what happened to my first guitar."

He motioned for the children to come closer. They gathered around and sat on the dirt.

"One day I was out in the field planting some potatoes when I heard a ruckus back at the ranch. I heard a gunshot. I thought maybe Ma or Pa or one of my little sisters and brothers might be in trouble, so I ran faster than Blue Lightning can gallop back to the house. I slowed down when I got there because I could hear an outlaw on the porch. He was tellin' Ma and Pa to hand over all their money or else he was going to steal our milk cow. I had to do something because I sure didn't want him to steal Ol' Bessie and I even surer didn't want him to shoot anyone. I peeked around the corner and listened. I could tell he had his back to me. I reached out for my guitar which I had left leaning against the porch rail. So as quiet as Mitch the mouse I stepped onto the porch, grabbed my guitar and I bashed the outlaw over the head! He dropped his gun and fell right down onto the porch. Then one of my little brothers rode into town and brought the sheriff back. As it turned out, the outlaw was wanted for robbing a bank in Arizona and there was a hundred dollar reward for capturing him. The sheriff gave us the reward money, and Pa bought me a new guitar. That money was enough to last for over a year, and the next Christmas there were presents under a bigger tree for all my younger brothers and sisters."

The kids roared and the adults applauded. He sang two more songs and then got back up on Blue Lightning.

"Well, I'm mighty sorry, but that's all the time I have today, little buckaroos."

He waved his hat as Blue Lightning reared up and pawed the air to say goodbye.

"I'm Tex Miller, the last of the singing cowboys, and maybe I'll be back to Healy City real soon."

He turned his horse and cantered away. The crowd could hear him singing as he rode out of town.

"I'm the last of the singing cowboys. Singin' songs of inspiration and joy."

The Last Cattle Round-Up

—◆—

"I want to say howdy to all my podners and all the little buckaroos who came out to see me today. I am Tex Miller, the last of the singing cowboys, and this is my horse Blue Lightning."

Tex hopped off his horse and faced the crowd of mostly young boys and girls in the town of Sierra Valley.

"I'm sure glad to be here today in Sierra Valley. Me and Blue have been traveling all through this fine state of California for a while now. Would you like to see Blue perform?"

The boys and girls shouted loud enough so Blue did some of his tricks.

"Blue, Mitch and I thank you for your kind applause. Now if you all will gather round and listen real quiet I will tell you a story."

The children sat down and listened.

"California is where I grew up. I lived on a small ranch just like I'm sure some of you do now. I worked on the ranch until I was fourteen-years-old, then I headed to Texas to become a real cowboy. I had had heard lots of stories about cowboys and how they rounded up all the cattle and went on long cattle drives up to Kansas Territory. I wanted to experience that for myself, so I said goodbye to Ma, Pa and all my little brothers and sisters. Then I packed up my horse and headed over the mountains and through the desert until I reached Texas. I found a job at a huge ranch called the Bar Twins. I did all the dirty, dusty jobs that the young cowboys needed to do to learn how to become a real cowboy. It was hard work, but I learned a lot and grew up straight, tall and strong. At night us cowboys would sit around a campfire outside the bunkhouse, and I would listen to the older cowboys tell stories about the cattle drives they had been on thirty or forty years ago. Before we all went to sleep, I would sing some of my songs. Would you like to hear some now?"

They clapped enough for Tex to sing his songs. He put his guitar back behind his saddle.

"Thank you for the kind attention. Now I'll tell you about the last cattle round-up that happened in the west part of Texas. By this time the railroad was finally getting close to the Bar Twins ranch outside of Telegraph Junction and all the ranch owners were shipping their cattle on the railroad. Mr. Kirby Jasper owned the ranch and he wanted us cowboys to have one last cattle drive before our old way of life disappeared. So we cowboys got ready. The ol' cook who had been going on cattle drives since he was knee high to a grasshopper loaded up his chuck wagon and we rounded up all Mr. Jasper's cattle. We set out for Abilene, Kansas, just like all the old cattle drives did. By day we would move the herd a few miles, and at night we would settle them down. We would eat our beans, biscuits and gravy and once in a while Cookie would make a stew out of rabbits or whatever he could catch. Once night he even made a pie out of raisins, flour and sugar. It didn't taste real good, but it was the first pie I had eaten since I left home. We would sit around the campfire and I'd listen to the old-timers tell their stories. One of my favorites was about the time a gang of rustlers tried to steal the herd. They stampeded the cattle in the middle of the night by firing their six-shooters and making a big racket. That woke up all the cowboys and they chased the rustlers for over a hundred miles before they caught them all and turned them over to the sheriff. Then they had to round up all the cattle. By the time they did that, it was close to fall. They finally made it to Abilene, but on the way back to Texas, they got caught in a blizzard. Now to hear that ol' cowboy tell the story, he claimed it snowed so hard for about a week that by the time they next saw the sun, there was over ten feet of snow in the valley. He said they had to dig a tunnel to get to the next town. Do you believe his story?"

The kids shook their heads and said no.

"Well, I didn't believe it either, until..."

He paused, held up a finger and whispered these words.

"When I was coming back from that last cattle round-up, it started snowing. We were back in Texas up in the mountains and it snowed so hard you couldn't see a match burning in front of your face. We had to make camp and hunker down for three days. When the snow stopped and the sun came out again, I looked around and all I could see of the chuck wagon was the very top of the canvas that covered it. We didn't have to dig a tunnel, but we had to dig a path for the wagon. That's how the last round-up ended. Now who would like to hear a song?"

The kids shouted and the adults clapped and a few men even whistled. He sang four more songs and then got back up on Blue Lightning.

"Well, that's all the time I have today."

He waved his hat as Blue Lightning reared up and pawed the air to say goodbye.

"I'm Tex Miller, the last of the singing cowboys, and maybe I'll be back to Sierra Valley real soon."

He turned his horse and they loped away. The crowd could hear him singing as he rode out of town.

"I'm the last of the singing cowboys. Singin' songs of inspiration and joy."

A Visit To Kinmundy Junction

—◆—

My name is Ken McGee and I'll tell you a story from long ago. One day I was sitting in my recliner and sorting through a box of old black and white photographs I hadn't seen for over fifty years. All of them taken in the small town of Kinmundy Junction where I lived as a child. I pulled another one out of the box and glanced at it. A man held a guitar as he sat astride a horse. At first, I thought it might be a photo of one of my uncles or even Grandpa. I looked closer and realized that was not the case. I smiled, leaned back and closed my eyes as I allowed my mind to drift back in time.

"Son, would you like to go into town with me?" Dad asked on a Saturday morning, as I lay on the floor in the living room listening to *The Lone Ranger* on the Philco radio.

"Can we go after this?" I didn't want to miss a moment of my favorite show.

"All right, but we will need to hurry."

The program signed off with the usual "Hi-Yo, Silver, away!" I jumped up and let Dad know I was ready.

"We'll be back in about an hour or two." He kissed Mom's cheek.

We often walked the half mile into town. Dad said we needed to save the gas for important trips. I didn't mind walking. I shielded my eyes against the sun in the cloudless sky as I ran ahead on the dusty, dirt road. I picked up a pebble and tossed it into the thick woods that crept close to the road. Dad chuckled as I scattered three female pheasants.

Thirty minutes later, we arrived in town. I looked down the main street. The only paved street in town.

"Why are there so many people here?" I had never seen so many people, except at church on Easter Sunday.

"It's a surprise. Someone special is coming to town."

"Who?" My curiosity overwhelmed me. I couldn't imagine who would draw everyone in town to the main street.

We walked closer and stopped outside of Jess Whitney's general store. Dad said howdy to a bunch of men in faded, dirty overalls. I watched as one of them spit his tobaccy into a rusty coffee can at his bare feet.

"Looks like the whole durn town is here," one of the men mentioned.

"Look! I think I can see him," another shouted.

"Who's coming?" I asked. "Pa, I can't see anything."

He picked me up and sat me on his shoulders. Everyone stared as a man on a large black and white horse trotted into town. He held onto the reins with one hand and waved a battered cowboy hat as his horse reared up on his hind legs.

"Is that the Lone Ranger?" I asked, as I frantically waved my hands to catch his attention.

"Just listen," Dad said as he patted my knee.

The ol' cowboy waved his hat as his horse pranced closer to the crowd of people. One of the men in dusty overalls grabbed the reins and the horse stopped right in front of us. I thought the cowboy looked right at me as he spoke.

"Howdy, y'all! My name is Tex Miller an this is Blue Lightning, and I'm the last of the singing cowboys."

The whole crowd of about thirty cheered, even the old men in their dirty overalls. He talked for a couple of minutes about cattle round-ups and sitting around a campfire at night singing songs.

"Would you like to hear a song?" He pulled a guitar

91

from behind his saddle and strummed it a couple of times. "How about *Back In The Saddle Again*? Do you know that one?"

The crowd hollered, then got real quiet as he started to sing, "I'm back in the saddle again. Out where a friend is a friend..."

I listened as he sang four or five songs, then a man put his guitar away for him.

"Who would like to see Blue Lightning show off some of his tricks?"

I hollered loud enough to bust Dad's eardrums. He had his horse do a 'rithmetic problem and then box an outlaw. Then he pulled out two apples and made Blue Lightning choose the red one. It was funny because neither of the two apples was red. One was yellow and the other was green. His horse knocked both apples out of his hand and they flew into the air toward us. I almost caught the yellow one, but I flew over my head. Then Tex pulled a red one out from under his ten-gallon Stetson hat and Blue Lightning ate it.

"Well, it's been good to see y'all, but I gots to mosey on down the road."

I could swear he pointed right at me and said, "Now y'all be good cowboys and cowgirls and listen to your Ma and Pa, y'hear. Mind your manners and be extra good to all the widows and orphans."

I nodded as he turned his horse and pranced away. I could hear him singing as he rode out of town. "I'm the last of the singing cowboys. Singin' songs of inspiration and joy."

I opened my eyes and grinned, even as a tear escaped my eye. That was the first time I ever saw Tex Miller, the self-proclaimed last of the singing cowboys and his horse Blue Lightning. I saw him a few more times over the course of several years. The last time he came to Kinmundy Junction, I

92

stood tall enough to see him on my own. Then he disappeared. I remembered asking Dad several years later if he would ever return.

"No, Ol' Tex Miller won't be comin' back anymore. He passed on to that *cattle round-up in the sky.*"

I understood what that meant. "Well, I hope that Tex Miller is having a good time singing songs around a heavenly campfire." I fought back tears, then added, "Pa, do you think he's still blind?"

Check out these other titles by the author. Visit the website: kennethleemcgee.com

The Emmy's Story Series

1. We Were 'posed to Get Married
2. One Of The Guys
3. A New Friend
4. Did You Like the Ravioli Tonight?
5. Completely and Forever: A Wedding
6. It's Time To Go!
7. How Difficult Can It Be?
8. Forever... Isabella... Forever
9. The Forgettable Year
10. Turning Thirty
11. Hello, I'm James
12. Remember The Struggle
13. But God! I Write Songs
14. A Lifelong Dream
15. Gideon's Tree
16. New Priorities
17. Christmas Surprise

The Annie Mercer O'Dell Series

1. Roosevelt High
2. North Park College
3. Smoky Mountain Summer

The Rex Ford & Clay Horn Books

1. The Amazing Adventures Of Rex Ford & Clay Horn

Stand Alone Books

1. Growing Up In Kinmundy Junction
2. Grandpa, Lions and Kitty Cats: A Collection Of Short Stories For Children Of All Ages
3. The True Stories of Ol' Melvin, Obadiah, Perkins MacGhee and Other Characters

I remember my grandfather watching
Westerns on TV as he lay on the couch
in the living room of the farmhouse.
He would never miss an episode of
Gunsmoke, *Wagon Train*,
or any of his other numerous favorites.
My favorite was *The Lone Ranger*.
I loved the action compacted into thirty minutes.

I wrote the following story to approximate the
movie serials from the 30s and 40s.
I'm including part of the next
Rex Ford & Clay Horn book as a bonus.

Each of these short movie episodes
would end in a cliffhanger with the hero,
or the damsel in distress, in grave peril.
Those of you who are old enough to remember
a more innocent time, sit back, relax and follow me
back to those thrilling days of yesteryear.

CLAY HORN RECOVERS

A Rex Ford & Clay Horn Adventure

Chapter One

"What did you say?" Ol' Doc Kimball asked.

"I said he jest squeezed my hand," Clara Ford answered with a grin as wide as all of Texas.

Rex Ford slapped his white Stetson hat against his hip and hollered, "That means he t'ain't dead yet! I reckon it takes a whole lot more than a bullet in the shoulder from a wild shot by that no-good, yeller-bellied, scum-suckin' varmint Rufus Gaiter and gittin' bit in the other right arm by a Western Diamondback rattler to do in Clay Horn. Yessirree! It takes more'n that."

"Let me take another listen," Doc Kimball said.

He used his fancy doctorin' tool and leaned over Clay. He moved the gadget 'round and listened to Clay's heart and lungs and mebbe even his belly. Then he straightened up and gave us a big ol' smile.

"Tell me he t'ain't dead yet, Doc," I pleaded.

"He's hangin' on by a silk thread."

"So he's got a chance to pull through, right?" Clara asked.

"I reckon so. A man in his condition should be dead, but he ain't," Doc said. "Someone musta been prayin' some powerful prayers."

I looked at Clara and she smiled back at me using that sweet smile she always dun when she were a kid and wanted to git her way.

"I didn't want him to die."

"You were wantin' him to live so he could take you steppin' out," I said with a grin. "I knowed he was sweet on you, an' you is jest as sweet on him."

"I ain't sayin' yore wrong," she said with eyes that were sparklin' like all the stars in the desert sky 'round midnight out at the ranch.

"I reckon he t'ain't out of the woods yet, but he has taken a few steps toward the meadow," Doc said. "It's gonna take a few days fore we can say for sure he's gonna make it. We need to move him to a bed 'cause Mrs. Kimball will be wantin' her fancy eatin' table back before supper."

It took four of us to move Clay from the table back to the room and sit him down in the fancy feather bed. He only groaned once. So I figgered he was gittin' better.

It took three more days but in the mornin', he kinda made a noise and opened his eyes. Me'n Clara was sittin' by the fancy bed when it happened.

"How's you feelin', podner," I asked.

"I feel like I dun been dragged through a cactus field by an orn'ry cuss of a bull. What happened?"

"You got shot in the shoulder by that yeller-bellied Rufus Gaiter and then a rattler dun bit yore other right arm."

"I remember now. Did we git all the scum-suckers we was after?"

"Rufus Gaiter is deader than last years Thanksgiving turkey, and I seen the Lamesa Kid roll off'n the cliff."

"Did you see his dead body?" Clay asked.

I shook my head as I scratched my jaw. "Well, I didn't 'xactly look fer it. I reckoned a five hundred foot fall would kill him fer shore."

Chapter Two

"How are you feelin' today?" I asked Clay about a week later. He were still gittin' used to his sore shoulder, but the rattler bite were 'bout healed.

"My shootin' shoulder is still stiff, and I feel like a newborn mustang tryin' to run on wobbly legs," Clay answered.

"Ol' Doc Kimball said you is 'bout healed 'nuff to head back to Roarin' Plains with me'n Clara if you feel so inclined."

"When do you reckon you'll be headin' home?" he asked.

"Clara is missin' Ma summat mighty. She is shore ready to go. I figger since me'n you is Texas Rangers, we has gotsa git back to doin' our job of ketchin' cattle rustlers, horse thieves, bank robbers and other lowlife, scum-suckin' bull whackers."

"I reckon you be right, but I shore would like to make shore Clara gits home safe." He twisted the ends of his handlebar mustache and stole a look at her as she were heppin' Mrs. Kimball put together some biscuits. "I shore would like that a might big heep."